SOFIA MARTINEZ

Every Day Is Exciting

by Jacqueline Jules

illustrated by Kim Smith

PICTURE WINDOW BOOKS
a capstone imprint

Sofia Martinez is published by
Picture Window Books, a Capstone Imprint
1710 Roe Crest Drive
North Mankato, MN 56003
www.mycapstone.com

Library of Congress Cataloging-in-
Publication data is available on the
Library of Congress website

ISBN 978-1-5158-2343-8 (paperback)
ISBN 978-1-5158-2345-2 (eBook PDF)

Summary: When Sofia is around, every
moment of every day is exciting. This
spunky seven-year-old can even make
having the hiccups fun! Can you imagine
what kind of fun Sofia will have at her
first quinceañera or when the lights go
out? No matter what happens, it will be
memorable if Sofia is involved!

Designer: Aruna Rangarajan
Art Director: Kay Fraser

Printed and bound in the USA.
010781S18

TABLE OF CONTENTS

Sofia's Party Shoes

CHAPTER 1

New Party Shoes

Sofia loved her new party shoes. They were white with lots of sparkle.

"They are very pretty," Sofia's older sister Elena said.

"Sí," Sofia's other sister Luisa agreed.

"Put the zapatos back in the
box and in the closet," Mamá said.
"They need to stay clean for the
party tonight."

Tonight was their friend Liliana's quinceañera. The whole family was going.

Sofia was excited about going to a quinceañera. It was her first one! And she was really excited about wearing her new shoes. That made the party extra special.

Mamá, Elena, and Luisa left the room. Sofia planned to do what Mamá said. But she couldn't wait until that tonight.

"I want to try them on one more time," Sofia decided.

She checked the hallway for Mamá. The hall was empty. Sofia went back to the closet and opened the box.

"Blanco," Sofia said. "Just like my party dress. A perfect match!"

Sofia's party dress had a ruffled white skirt. It was pretty, but it was not new.

Elena had worn the party dress first. Luisa had worn it too. Only the party shoes were Sofia's alone.

"I want to show my cousins," Sofia thought. "They are just across the backyard. Nothing will happen on such a short walk."

Sofia peeked into the hallway to check for **Mamá** again. It was clear! Sofia tiptoed down the stairs and out the door.

CHAPTER 2

Purple Juice

There was grass in the yards between Sofia's house and her cousins' house.

She looked down at her shoes. They sparkled in the sunlight. Would the green grass stain her shoes?

Sofia didn't want to take the chance. She took the long way around, using the sidewalk.

She hopped over a melting lollipop. She carefully stepped past a muddy puddle.

And she slowly backed away from her neighbor's dog.

"Sorry, Bruno. I can't have dog slobber on me today," she said.

Sofia arrived at her cousins' house with perfectly white shoes. Hector led her into the kitchen. Alonzo, Manuel, and baby Mariela were all drinking grape juice with Tía Carmen.

"¡Mira!" Sofia said. "My new party shoes!"

"Están muy bonitos," Tía Carmen said.

"¡Gracias!" Sofia said.

Baby Mariela waved her cup and dropped it from her high chair. The cup rolled near Sofia's feet.

The top on the baby cup kept the juice inside. Close call! Sofia's shoes were safe!

Alonzo leaned over for Mariela's cup. As he did, his arm bumped Manuel's juice.

This cup didn't have a lid. Sofia tried to jump out of the way. But it was too late.

Purple liquid spilled all over Sofia's new white shoes!

"¡Qué pena!" Tía Carmen said.

"I'm so sorry," Alonzo said.

"It's not your fault," Sofia said. "I should have listened to **Mamá**."

Tía Carmen scrubbed and scrubbed the shoes. Then Sofia did the same. She scrubbed and scrubbed and scrubbed. But it was no use. The purple would not come off.

Sofia's new white party shoes were no longer white.

CHAPTER 3

The Party

Mamá shook her head when she saw Sofia's stained shoes. "You'll have to wear them like this," she said.

"Yo sé," Sofia said.

When it was time to go to the party, Elena and Luisa got into the backseat of the car. They were all dressed up and smiling.

Sofia was frowning. Her arms were folded.

"Don't be grumpy," Mamá said. "You can still have a good time."

"Sí," Papá agreed. "A quinceañera is a celebration."

At the church, Sofia cheered up. It was exciting to see Liliana in her beautiful quinceañera gown. The long dress was sky blue with glittering beads.

"She looks like a princess!" Sofia told Mamá.

"¡Claro!" Mamá said. "This is
an important birthday for Liliana.
She is fifteen years old."

Before the special waltz, Liliana sat in a fancy chair. Her father helped her change from flat shoes into high heels. Her shoes matched her blue dress exactly.

Sofia looked at her own shoes. They didn't match her dress at all. She sat down and took them off.

"Oh, Sofia," Elena said. "It's not that bad."

"Come on! Join the party!" Luisa added.

Fancy shoes are not comfortable to dance in. One by one the girls took off their shoes, just like Sofia. By the end of the night, there was a huge pile of shoes.

"Are these mine?" Elena asked.

"No," another girl said.

"They're mine."

"All the shoes look alike!"

Luisa complained.

"Not all of them!"

Sofia said.

She grabbed hers with a huge smile. "My shoes are easy to find!"

And that was the perfect way to end Sofia's first **quinceañera**.

Hector's Hiccups

CHAPTER 1

HIC!

Movie day was finally here!

Abuela was taking Sofia and her

cousin Hector. They were going to

see the movie *Jeffrey's Giant*.

They were all ready to go when they heard a loud noise.

"*HIC! HIC!*"

"What was that?" Abuela asked.

"*HIC!*"

"I think it was Hector," Sofia said.

"*HIC! HIC!*"

"Oh no! Hector has the hiccups!" Sofia said.

"*HIC! HIC!*" Hector replied.

"We should take care of this before the movie," Abuela said.

Abuela cut a slice of lemon. She gave it to Hector.

"This is what my abuela used to cure hiccups," she said.

It didn't work.

"*HIC! HIC!*"

"What about a glass of water?" Sofia said.

"Sí," Abuela agreed. "¡Agua!"

She gave Hector a glass. He took a big gulp.

"*HIC! HIC!*"

Water didn't work either.

"Nothing works! *HIC!*" Hector
said. "I'm going to have the
hiccups forever! *HIC! HIC!*"

"Just relax," Abuela said.

"Don't give up," Sofia said.
"Try to hold your breath. I'll do
it too."

Sofia and Hector held their
breath together.

"Uno, dos, tres, cuatro,
cinco . . ." Abuela counted.

After she reached ten, Abuela
waved her arms. Then she shouted,
"BOO!"

"HIC! HIC!"

Hector still had the hiccups.

"HIC! HIC!"

And now Sofia did too.

CHAPTER 2

Popcorn

"¡Ay dios mio!" Abuela said. "Now I have two children with hiccups."

"*HIC!*" Sofia answered.

"*HIC!*" Hector chimed in.

"Maybe we should watch a movie at home," Abuela said.

"*HIC!* What about popcorn?" Sofia asked.

"I really love popcorn," Hector added.

"We can make it ourselves," Abuela said.

Abuela took out a big pot. She poured a little oil in the bottom. She put three kernels of popcorn in the pot.

"Why only three?" Sofia asked. "Do we each only get one piece of popcorn?"

Abuela laughed. "The first three kernels are a test. That's how we know when the oil is hot enough to cook the rest."

She put a lid on the pot. Then they waited.

Sofia hiccupped twice. "*HIC! HIC!*"

Then it was Hector's turn. "*HIC! HIC! HIC!*"

A few minutes later, they heard another sound. *POP! POP! POP!*

Abuela poured in more kernels.

That's when it got very noisy.

POP! POP! HIC! POP! POP! POP!
HIC! HIC!

"It's like music!" Abuela raised
her arms. "¡Vamos a bailar!"

Sofia and Hector danced too.

POP! POP! POP! HIC! POP! HIC!
POP! POP! POP!

When the popcorn was ready,
Abuela poured it into a bowl. She
added salt and butter.

"¡Delicioso!" Sofia said.

It was still noisy, but not with

the same noise.

CRUNCH! CRUNCH! CRUNCH!

There were no more *POPS* or *HICS!*

"Yay!" Sofia cheered. "No more hiccups! Now we can go and see the movie."

Abuela looked at her watch. "We'll have to hurry."

CHAPTER 3

The Movie

The movie theater was not far, but there was a lot of traffic.

"Hurry, Abuela!" Sofia said.

"I'm going as fast as I can, sweet girl!" Abuela said.

When they got to the movie theater they had another problem.

"No parking spaces!" Hector said. "Now what?"

"Now we stay patient and calm and look for an open parking spot," **Abuela** said. "It's no use getting worked up."

Abuela drove around the parking lot once. Then she drove around again. And again. And again.

They finally found a spot in the very back.

"Hold my hands," **Abuela** said. "We'll run. **Vámonos!**"

They were out of breath when they bought their tickets. But they had five minutes to spare!

Abuela stopped and bought popcorn and drinks.

"But we already had popcorn," Hector said.

"You can never have too much popcorn," **Abuela** said.

Sofia, **Abuela**, and Hector settled in their seats. The lights went down and the music started.

"*HIC! HIC!*"

"Who was that?" Sofia asked.

"It wasn't me!" Hector said.

"*HIC!*"

It was **Abuela**!

"**Ay dios mio!**" she covered

her mouth. Sofia and Hector

just laughed.

Lights
Out

CHAPTER 1

No Lights

Sofia switched on the light in her bedroom. Nothing happened! She went into the hallway. The light didn't work there, either.

"¡Mamá!" she called.

"We are all downstairs," Mamá said.

Sofia found Mamá, Papá, and her two older sisters, Elena and Luisa, in the kitchen. They were listening to a radio.

"¿Qué pasa?" Sofia asked.

"There was a big storm last night," Elena said.

"The electricity is out," Luisa added.

"When will it come back?"

Sofia asked.

"We don't know," Papá said.

"The outage is widespread," the woman on the radio said. "Be prepared for a night without power."

"There's your answer, Sofia," Papá said.

"Oh no!" **Mamá** said, worried.

"The refrigerator will get warm.

All the food will go bad."

"Oh no! The yummy ice cream

will melt," Luisa said.

"No, it won't." Sofia opened the freezer. "We can eat it for breakfast."

Elena giggled. "Mamá and Papá will never let us do that."

"¿Por qué no?" Sofia said. "Is it better to throw it out?"

"Sofia has a point." Papá got spoons and bowls.

"Chocolate chip. My favorite!" Sofia said.

After the ice cream breakfast, everyone looked for flashlights. They only found one.

"Is this the only one we have?" Sofia asked.

"Sí," Mamá said.

Papá picked up his jacket.
"I better go to the store."

"Can I come?" Sofia asked.
"¿Por favor?"

"¡Vámonos!" Papá said,
smiling.

CHAPTER 2

A Bright Idea

When they got to the store, the man at the counter said, "We are out of ice and flashlights."

"It's going to be a dark night for us," Papá said.

But Sofia saw something else
they could use.

"Can we buy that pumpkin
candle?" she asked.

"Why would we need a
Halloween candle?" Papá asked.

"It will help us see tonight,"
Sofia said.

"You are one smart girl, Sofia!"
Papá said.

Sofia looked at all the Halloween
items. Lots of them glowed in the dark.

"Papá," she said as she looked at a big display. "Could we get some of those? I have an idea."

She whispered her idea to Papá. He smiled.

"Muy bien. The family will have fun," he said.

On the way home, Papá stopped by Abuela's.

"I don't have any electricity," Abuela said.

"Come home with us," Sofia said. "We are having a cookout."

"Family should be together when the power is out," Papá said. "Nobody should be alone in the dark."

"Gracias," Abuela said. "It is no fun to be in the dark."

"It could be," Sofia grinned.

Papá grinned too.

"What are you two planning?" Abuela asked.

"Just wait and see," Sofia said.

Back at home, Sofia walked across the yard to talk to her cousin Hector.

"Can you bring your new drums over tonight?" she asked.

"Sí," Hector said. "Anything else you need?"

They searched the toy box. They found Manuel's fire truck and baby Mariela's duck on wheels.

"Alonzo has something good too," Hector said. "I'll bring it."

Sofia rubbed her hands together. "Perfecto."

CHAPTER 3

Dancing in the Dark

That night, Hector's family packed up and headed to Sofia's house for dinner.

"An October cookout!" Tío Miguel said. "It's just like summer!"

"Not even close," Hector said as he shivered.

"It is a little cold. Let's go inside," Tía Carmen said. "I think it's almost time to eat."

"Thank goodness," Hector said. "I'm hungry and cold."

"I think we are all hungry and cold," Tío Miguel said.

They headed inside to join the rest of the family.

There were twelve people
around the table, including baby
Mariela in her high chair.

Mamá lit the pumpkin candle,
but the food was still hard to see.

It was not a normal family dinner, but everyone made the best of the situation.

Abuela told stories. Tío Miguel told jokes. And baby Mariela babbled and cried.

After dinner, everyone cleaned up. It was a little tricky in the dark.

Then Sofia invited everyone into the living room. She couldn't wait to show them her big surprise!

Papá held up a sheet like a
curtain. Sofia disappeared behind
it and counted to three.

¡Uno . . . dos . . . tres!

"Ta-da!" Sofia yelled as she jumped out.

She was wearing glowing rings, bracelets, and earrings. She danced while Hector banged his toy drums. The drums had battery lights.

Mamá lit a candle on the
piano. Then she sat down and
played a salsa. Elena and Luisa
clapped.

"Time to dance!" they yelled.

Tía Carmen grabbed Tío Miguel's hand. They started dancing. Tío Miguel was not a good dancer, so it was extra funny.

Papá gave out glow-in-the-dark necklaces. Baby Mariela dragged her duck with the light-up wheels. Manuel switched on his fire truck. Alonzo waved his light saber.

Abuela sang and danced too. She waved her glow-in-the-dark necklace in the air.

Then suddenly, the lights flickered. Everyone stopped. Then the lights flickered again. Suddenly, the room was filled with light.

"Hooray! The lights are back on!" Hector shouted.

"Turn them off!" Sofia cried.

"I'm already on my way to the light switch," **Abuela** said, smiling.

And just like that, the room was dark again.

Spanish Glossary

abuela — grandmother

agua — water

ay dios mío — oh my goodness

blanco — white

claro — of course

delicioso — delicious

están muy bonitos — they are very pretty

gracias — thank you

mamá — mom

mira — look

muy bien — very good

papá — dad

perfecto — perfect

por favor — please

por qué no — why not

qué pena — too bad

qué pasa — what's wrong

quinceañera — celebration of a girl's fifteenth birthday

sí — yes

tía — aunt

tío — uncle

uno, dos, tres, cuatro, cinco — one, two, three, four, five

vámonos — let's go

vamos a bailar — let's dance

yo sé — I know

zapatos — shoes

About the Author

Jacqueline Jules is the award-winning author of more than forty children's books, including *No English* (2012 Forward National Literature Award), *Zapato Power: Freddie Ramos Takes Off* (2010 CYBILS Literary Award, Maryland Blue Crab Young Reader Honor Award, and ALSC Great Early Elementary Reads), and *Freddie Ramos Makes a Splash* (named on 2013 List of Best Children's Books of the Year by Bank Street College Committee).

When not reading, writing, or teaching, Jacqueline enjoys time with her family in Northern Virginia.

About the Illustrator

Kim Smith has worked in magazines, advertising, animation, and children's gaming. She studied illustration at the Alberta College of Art and Design in Calgary, Alberta.

Kim is the illustrator of the upcoming middle-grade mystery series *The Ghost and Max Monroe,* the picture book *Over the River and Through the Woods*, and the cover of the forthcoming middle-grade novel *How to Make a Million*. She resides in Calgary, Alberta.

See you soon!

¡Nos vemos pronto!

www.capstonekids.com